PUFFIN BOOKS

NEVER KISS FROGS!

Gail's life isn't much like a fairy story. She and her mum live in the basement of their house and take in lodgers to make ends meet. If Gail could just kiss a frog who happened to be a rich prince in disguise, their troubles would be over.

Then one day, Gail does find her enchanted frog and, whoosh, Prince Rupert appears. The only trouble is he doesn't have any money or a castle, just a huge appetite and lots of dirty washing. Gail's mother falls for him in a big way, so it takes Aunt Mandy to sort him out; she knows all about princes and frogs.

The next time Gail hears a frog talking to her, she's not so keen on the kissing part. Princess Edwina is bossy, conceited and a know-it-all. Even worse, she used to be engaged to Prince Rupert in a previous life, and now she wants to take him away from Gail's mum. Luckily, Aunt Mandy is on hand to save the day again.

These two sparklingly funny stories, *Never Kiss Frogs!*, and its sequel, *One Frog Too Many*, are published together in one edition for double the fun.

Robert Leeson has been an author and journalist for many years, and has written more than thirty books for young people. In 1985 he was awarded the Eleanor Farjeon award for services to children and literature.

By the same author

PANCAKE PICKLE

Robert Leeson

Never Kiss Frogs!

Illustrated by David Simonds

PUFFIN BOOKS

PUFFIN BOOKS

Published by the Penguin Group
Penguin Books Ltd, 27 Wrights Lane, London W8 5TZ, England
Penguin Books USA Inc., 375 Hudson Street, New York, New York 10014, USA
Penguin Books Australia Ltd, Ringwood, Victoria, Australia
Penguin Books Canada Ltd, 10 Alcorn Avenue, Toronto, Ontario, Canada M4V 3B2
Penguin Books (NZ) Ltd, 182–190 Wairau Road, Auckland 10, New Zealand

Penguin Books Ltd, Registered Offices: Harmondsworth, Middlesex, England

Never Kiss Frogs! first published by Hamish Hamilton 1988
One Frog Too Many first published by Hamish Hamilton 1991
Published in one volume in Puffin Books 1992
1 3 5 7 9 10 8 6 4 2

Text copyright © Robert Leeson, 1988, 1991
Illustrations copyright © David Simonds, 1988, 1991
All rights reserved

The moral right of the author has been asserted

Printed in England by Clays Ltd, St Ives plc
Filmset in Baskerville

Contents

Never Kiss Frogs!

Chapter One

Gail was a nice girl. Sometimes she behaved well. Sometimes she behaved badly. Sometimes she worked hard. Sometimes she was idle. Sometimes she got on with her friends. Sometimes she had a row with them. She was just about average, was Gail.

But there was one thing different about her.

She had one funny habit.

Gail kissed frogs.

Well, she tried. It's not all that

easy. It seems easy enough. Frogs sit there very quiet under a stone or a leaf. They don't move. They don't even blink when you look at them. And, their lips stick out a bit, as though they're waiting for someone to give them a big kiss.

But you try and do it.

For one thing, you have to get your face down two inches off the ground. It's very awkward, but that's the way frogs are made.

The trouble is, once you've got down on your knees, and got your face nice and close, what do they do?

They jump. They jump about three feet, not all that far but a long way for a frog. And it doesn't half put you off if you're trying to kiss one.

But Gail kept trying because she'd read in a book somewhere that when a girl kissed a frog, he turned into a prince. A prince with a castle and about two thousand bags of gold and a father who's just about to pop off and leave his kingdom. Then, there's a big wedding, because the prince is grateful and wants to reward the girl

who kissed him, and they all live
happily ever after.

And Gail was quite keen on living
happily ever after. There were times
when she was fed up with life. She
lived at home with her mother. Her
dad wasn't around, and her mother
had to work hard to keep them both.
To make a proper living, they took in
lodgers. So Gail and her mother lived

in the basement and the lodgers lived upstairs. There was a lot of cooking and washing and cleaning. It went on most evenings and every weekend.

Sometimes Gail helped her mother. Sometimes she didn't feel like it. So her mother would just shrug her shoulders and go on working. Then Gail would feel awful and go and help her.

So, every now and then Gail wished that just for once they could have a house all to themselves and enough money not to have to fry bacon and sausage, and wash up, and take loads of dirty washing down to the launder-ette for other people.

Sometimes, when she was fed up, Gail would go out in the garden at the back. It was a sort of garden. Every now and then her mum would go berserk with spades and forks and rakes. Then she'd give up and the grass would grow back, the weeds would sprout and the place would look like Tarzan's back yard again.

Chapter Two

One day, Gail had a row with her mother. She went out into the garden for a sulk. There'd been a shower and the sun had just come out again. Everything was damp and steamy. As Gail got to the bottom of the garden and looked round for something to kick, she suddenly had the feeling that someone was watching her. She looked around — there was no one there. But Gail knew she was being watched.

Then she saw it. Sitting under a dock leaf, big beady eyes staring, breathing in and out, was the biggest, fattest, grottiest-looking frog. For a moment or two they looked at each other, then the frog spoke.

"Sweet lady. Please have pity on me."

"You what?" said Gail. She didn't

mean to be rude. Her mother was always trying to get her to say "Beg pardon". But it just came out.

"Have pity on a poor creature in distress," said the frog.

Gail crouched down and very carefully put her face a few inches from the frog's. But it didn't move. Instead it spoke again.

"My story," said the frog, "is a long and sad one . . ."

But Gail couldn't wait. She knew what she had to do. She squeezed up her mouth and gave the frog a great big kiss right in the middle of his sentence.

There was a sudden noise like the sound of a blown-up paper bag bursting. Then Gail found herself staring

not at the frog any more, but at a pair
of highly polished leather boots.

Standing in front of her was a tall,
handsome man, with wavy blonde
hair and sky blue eyes, dressed in the
most stunning red and gold uniform.

"Oh great," breathed Gail. "A real
prince. Smashing."

She spread out her arms, went down on one knee and said, "Your humble servant, your Highness."

The prince looked down at her, raised his eyebrows and said, "Oh, blow."

"You wha — I mean, I beg your pardon, your gracious . . ."

"I mean," said the Prince, "you're a bit younger than I expected . . ."

"I'm nearly eleven," retorted Gail, a little more sharply than she meant to. "I'm starting at Hob Lane Comprehensive this autumn."

"Comprehensive?"

The prince looked baffled. Gail didn't try to explain. She guessed he'd never been to a comprehensive school anyway. She was a bit put out, now.

"What's wrong with me? I kissed you, didn't I? I broke the spell. What more did you want?"

The Prince drew himself up a little further.

"There is no need to be impertinent. I am, of course, grateful for your help. But according to the rules I am supposed to marry you. And to be quite frank, you are under age."

"Gail!" Mum was calling from the basement window. "Will you come in? It's going to start raining any minute."

"Won't be a minute, Mum," Gail shouted back. She was thinking fast. This wasn't turning out as she expected. It'd be another five years at least before she could marry the Prince. And how was she going to keep him hanging about till then? She played for time.

"Your Highness. My name is Gail." She waved a hand. "This is our humble abode. Would you care to partake of . . ." She tried to think what they were having for supper and what the posh name for it was. Fish-burgers — oh no.

"You — Gail!" Gail nearly jumped out of her skin. Her mother was standing right by her. For a moment Gail thought the Prince was going to be invisible. But no such luck.

"Who's this? And what's he doing in fancy dress? Is he looking for a room? The top one's empty."

At the sound of her voice, the Prince turned round and looked straight at Gail's mother. She blushed and started patting her hair.

Oh no, thought Gail, this is getting complicated.

"Er, Prince — I'm afraid I don't know your name. This is my mother."

"Prince Rupert," answered the man. "But, surely not your mother. Perhaps your sister."

Oh, he's one of those, thought Gail. She looked at her mother again, who was going all soppy.

"I'm Jackie, short for Jacqueline," said Mum, her voice going squeaky with embarrassment. "Would you like to come in for a cup of tea?" Mum pulled herself together and started taking charge. They walked towards the back door and Gail trailed along behind. This was not turning out right at all.

Chapter Three

Things got worse. Prince Rupert had a very hearty appetite. He ate six fishburgers (there were only eight in the packet), and drank seven cups of tea. There was hardly anything left for Gail and her mum, but her mum didn't seem to notice.

Prince Rupert chatted on about life at court, how big the castle was, how many servants, how his father was just about to retire. He explained how happy he'd been until a wicked witch had taken a dislike to the family and put a spell on him. And ever since he'd been living as a frog in this damp hole in the ground.

Huh, thought Gail, this basement isn't much better. The point was how soon could they move into the castle? That's what she wanted to know. But every time she wanted to ask an important question like that, her mum said, "Please don't interrupt, Gail. You were saying, Prince Rupert?"

And Prince Rupert seemed to have forgotten completely which fair maiden had rescued him.

In fact, thought Gail, she was beginning to go off Prince Rupert.

Suddenly she knew what was going to happen. Mum was going to marry Prince Rupert, and she was going to be a prince's step-daughter. That wasn't so good. Gail knew what happened to step-daughters in fairy tales. It was about time she sorted things out.

"I say," she burst out. "I say" is the posh way you interrupt people. "I say."

Mum and Prince Rupert both stopped talking and looked at her.

"Where is this castle of yours?"

"Why, just a half mile away," answered Prince Rupert.

"Well, there's no castle for miles round here," declared Gail.

"Don't be so rude, Gail," said her mother. But Prince Rupert looked baffled.

"Perhaps," he said loftily, "the wicked witch has enchanted the castle away."

Just my luck, thought Gail. But she wasn't giving up yet. "Where is your father's kingdom, then?"

"Why, all around as far as a man can ride in seven days and seven nights."

"You're joking. This is Westchester," retorted Gail, "and we ought to know. We've lived here all our lives."

Prince Rupert went red in the face.

"How dare you contradict me?" He stood up. "I shall not stay here a moment longer, in this hovel. I shall return to the castle immediately."

Mum jumped up and grabbed the Prince by the arm.

"Now, please, your Highness, do calm down. I'm sure no offence was meant. Please stay the night. I have a room empty."

"There's only the box room," said Gail.

"No there's not," snapped her mother. "The others can all move up one and he can have the best room."

Prince Rupert sat down. "Very well. I will stay the night. And out of gratitude, I shall forget your daughter's impertinence."

Gail was ready to explode. But her mother had already gone to sort things out. The lodgers didn't like it, but before they knew it, they were all shifted up one room and Prince Rupert was fixed up in the best room.

Mum even found an old pair of pyjamas for him.

So Prince Rupert stayed the night, and the next night and the next. He stayed in bed until the afternoon most days and then he would get up for supper, eat a lot, drink some wine or a

bottle of beer, talk a lot about life at court and go to bed again. The lodgers thought it was a bit of a giggle at first, but in the end they got fed up with hearing his stories and went off down the pub.

They got even more fed up because Mum was so busy seeing to Prince Rupert, that she didn't bother about cooking their meals properly or clean-

ing the house — apart from the best room. After a while the other lodgers moved out. They'd had enough of hearing Prince Rupert telling them, "So, I said to the Grand Duke . . ."

But things got worse. Mum was so busy looking after Prince Rupert, laundering and ironing his uniform every day, polishing his boots and serving breakfast and lunch in bed, that she was later and later for work until she got the sack. But she didn't seem to notice.

The rest of the house got emptier and dustier. The weeds and grass in the garden grew like triffids. Prince Rupert lay in bed and called for his breakfast and his supper and his polished boots, and Mum ran to and fro whenever he called.

She began to look so pale and thin that Gail stopped feeling furious with her and began to feel worried. After a few weeks, Mum suddenly got 'flu and had to stay in bed. She didn't really want to, but Gail made her.

Gail stopped off school to look after things. But after two days of Prince

Rupert, and his 'Bring me this, bring me that', she'd had enough. That evening, when Mum was tucked up in bed and Prince Rupert was sitting noshing fried chicken in the best room Gail 'phoned Aunt Mandy. Aunt Mandy was tall and slim like Mum, but just a bit different in her ways. She drove a van for the local council and when she cornered, the old folk would say 'Here comes meals on two wheels'.

Chapter Four

Aunt Mandy arrived early next day and went through the house like a dose of salts. She marched into the best room. Gail closed her ears but she could still hear the banging and shouting. Then Aunt Mandy came out with that lovely red uniform under her arm.

"Right, Gail, stuff that lot in the boiler will you."

Suddenly Prince Rupert appeared

in the doorway, in his underpants. He looked truly ridiculous.

"Where is my uniform, woman?" he demanded.

"Just going up in smoke, your worship", answered Aunt Mandy. "Here." From out of her bag she pulled a pair of jeans and an old shirt. "Now get these on and get out in that garden and start cutting that grass."

Prince Rupert went the colour of his trousers.

"How dare you, you impudent witch."

Aunt Mandy took two steps towards him.

"Do you think I'm a witch?" she said, grinning a wicked grin.

Prince Rupert's face turned the

colour of his underpants. Without another word he took the shirt and jeans. He marched off to his room.

"I shall certainly not cut the grass. Get a gardener," he said.

Aunt Mandy put her hands on her hips. "No grass, no breakfast, mate," she said.

Prince Rupert stuck it out until supper time. But next day when Gail came home from school, the garden

was cleared, all the weeds were pulled up. It hadn't looked so good for years. Inside the kitchen Aunt Mandy and Prince Rupert were having a cup of tea. He had a bandage on his hand. Gail felt quite sorry for him.

"Oh, did you cut your hand on the shears?" she asked.

"No, love, he burnt it making a cup of tea. But he's shaping," said Aunt Mandy.

So, it all turned out not too badly after all. Mum got better. She got her job back. And Prince Rupert got a part-time job at the Bingo Club. When he called out, "All the sevens" in that posh voice of his, the old ladies loved it.

They didn't earn much, but it was enough for the three of them. And they didn't bother with lodgers any more. So Gail was able to live in the whole house after all. She got to quite like Rupert in the end — though not as much as her mum did.

So they all lived happily ever after.

Then one day, after it had been raining, Gail was out in the garden pulling up the odd weed in the flower bed. As she bent down, she had the feeling someone was watching her.

And there under the azalea sat the biggest, fattest, grottiest-looking frog you ever saw, gazing at her with his great, beady eyes.

Then he spoke.

"Sweet lady. Have pity on me."

Gail looked him straight in the eye. "Listen, buster. You have one minute to get out of here."

One Frog Too Many

For Katie

Chapter One

Gail and her mother lived in an old
house with three floors and a long
back garden. They used to have
lodgers but since Rupert came to
stay, the lodgers went. Then there
were just the three of them.

Rupert was tall and handsome and
had a fruity voice. The old girls at
the Bingo Club where he worked
just loved it. He was useful round the
house too. He hadn't always been.
When he first arrived he was a bit

idle and talked too much. But with a little help from Aunt Mandy he was shaping. And Gail quite got to like him.

Not as much as Mum did, though. She thought he was her dream come true. The atmosphere in the house was so romantic, Gail found it a bit boring. She'd run into them here and there, clinching in the kitchen, smooching on the stairway. She couldn't get to watch important programmes on the telly because they were staring at old films, holding hands and chewing chocolates.

"I don't see why they don't get married," she told Aunt Mandy.

"Oh, I reckon your mum's quite

keen," her aunt replied. "But Rupert's a bit evasive. You know — quite happy as I am. Why all the formality. That sort of talk."

"You're not married," said Gail.

Aunt Mandy grinned.

"I prefer living on my own. Blokes do clutter up the house. But marriage is OK, with the right feller. Anyway, perhaps something may happen to make Rupert change his mind."

When Rupert had tidied up the garden last year, he went berserk and built a pond. And filled it with goldfish. It looked great.

Then one night in spring, Gail heard this funny noise: "Ark-ark,

ark-ark." She guessed what it was. Sure enough, before long on the surface of the little pond was a lot of spotted jelly.

"Frog spawn," said Mum. "It'll have to go."

Rupert didn't answer, but Gail said, "Oh, why?"

"Can't have bullheads – tadpoles," said Mum. "The little devils get so hungry they might start eating the fish. You'll have to scoop

them out, Rupert love. What's up, lad?" she asked as Rupert turned green.

Rupert said nothing. Gail knew what was wrong with him. Rupert had a secret which Gail and Aunt Mandy shared. Rupert had once been a Frog-Prince. Gail had rescued him last summer with a well-timed kiss. Mum didn't know this. She thought Rupert dropped into her life from a passing cloud. And she wasn't interested in the past, but more in the present – and future.

"All right, all right," said Gail. "I'll see to the bullheads."

She got a bucket, fished out the tadpoles and carried them off to school. Everyone in Class Four crowded round as Miss took some of the frog spawn for the aquarium.

"There's something in there," said Sheree, one of Gail's crowd. "You scooped up a frog as well."

"Let's keep it," shouted Class Four.

But Miss shook her head. "We'll have enough frogs of our own later on. We can watch them grow. But this is one frog too many. It can go in Maggie's pond together with the rest of the spawn."

And so it did.

Chapter Two

As spring moved on, the tadpoles, all
head and tail, hatched out. At home,
Rupert and Mum cuddled and fell
out and were generally boring.
Grown-ups often behave like
children, thought Gail, one day as
she sat on the grass bank at the top
of the school yard. She was alone.
The sun shone, new leaves sprouted
on the trees and the noise in the
playground seemed far away.

Then someone spoke, quite close
to her.

"You there!"

Gail turned round. She could see
no one. This voice seemed to come
from the grass.

"Wake up. Are you a prince or a
princess – a boy or a girl?"

The voice was very bossy. Gail
was puzzled. She looked around,
then spotted the frog crouching

among the oak tree roots, lean, green
and smooth, beady eyes staring at
her haughtily.

"I'm a girl, of course," she
answered.

"Well, what are you wearing
trousers for?"

"Mind your own business,"
retorted Gail.

"Don't be impertinent. I can tell
by your manners you're no princess.
In any case, you're a girl and that's
worse than useless."

"You watch it . . ." snapped Gail.

The frog ignored the threat. "I am
Princess Edwina," she announced.

"So?" Gail was not impressed.

"A wicked witch turned me into a
frog and . . ."

60

"That's an old story," Gail said carelessly.

"Don't interrupt. I am looking for someone to – ah, help me. A male someone . . ."

"Well," said Gail, "there's Gareth down there, or Grunter . . ."

She didn't mention Boxer because she wasn't going to let any pushy frog kiss him.

The frog sprang up on to the tree root and surveyed the school yard.

"They all look like peasants to me. I need a prince of the blood royal," she said haughtily.

"We've . . ." Gail began, then stopped. She was going to say, "We've got a prince at home . . ." But she didn't trust this frog.

She went on, "We've only got one Royal Family in Britain, and they're miles away."

"What a way to run a country," murmured Edwina.

She hopped down off the root.

"Well, make yourself useful, girl. Get a bucket, some damp grass or leaves and a worm or two for the journey."

"What journey?" asked Gail, baffled.

"You shall have the honour of transporting me back to the nice suburban pond from which I was so rudely taken last month."

Chapter Three

Back at home that afternoon, Rupert had arrived early and was sitting on the garden bench with his arm around Mum.

So Gail took the bucket and Edwina up to her room. The frog seemed to have survived the journey well.

"Come on girl, help me out."

"My name's Gail. And I'm not your servant, you stuck-up madam," she answered sharply.

To her surprise, Edwina chuckled.

"I ought to have you soundly thrashed for your insolence. But that will have to wait. Place me on the window sill and raise the sash for me to look out. That will do. Careful!"

As the window sash went up, Rupert and Mum turned, blushed, then waved.

"Who is that handsome person?"

"That's my mum."

"No, idiot child. The male person."

"Oh, that's our Rupert."

"Rupert. How very interesting."

The back door banged below them.

"Now where have they gone? I can't see them."

Gail shrugged. "In the kitchen, I expect."

"The kitchen? What for?"

"Oh, they'll be doing the washing-up, making tea."

"What? Both of them?"

"Yes, why not?" demanded Gail.

"Washing-up?" shrieked Edwina. "What a way to treat a . . ." She stopped, then sighed.

Gail got up from her bed where she had been sitting.

"Before you go down – er Gail," Edwina's voice became coaxing. "Just get me a wet flannel to sit on and leave the window and the door open."

"What for?" asked Gail, suspiciously.

"I must have fresh air," said
Edwina. "And, I'd love a nice fat
slug for my supper."

That evening Mum was out for her evening class, so Rupert and Gail spent a quiet time together. He bought a can of beer for himself, and coke and crisps for Gail. They watched telly for a bit, but it was pretty ropey; tired old sitcoms, a programme about the decline of Royalty and another one about flying frogs in Australia. Rupert looked uneasy and switched off.

So they chatted a bit about this

and that. Rupert told Gail how he
liked staying with her and Mum and
how grateful he was to Gail for
having rescued him from his frog-life.

Gail took the bull by the horns.

"Are you and Mum getting
married?" she asked.

Rupert looked embarrassed, then
serious.

"You know, Gail, in my life,
before," he waved his hand towards
the back garden. "I was going to be

married. It had all been arranged by our parents when we were quite small. That's how Royals do it. I had no choice. I hated it. She was so conceited. Such a know-all."

"Ah," said Gail, beginning to understand everything. "What was her name?"

"Edwina."

"Ah," said Gail again.

Chapter Four

Things speeded up. At school the
tadpoles were changing. Their tails
shrank and they began to put out
arms and legs. Class Four began to
bet on how soon they'd be fully
paid-up frogs.

At home, Edwina seemed quite
happy to live in the bucket under
Gail's bed, or to lie on a wet flannel
on the window sill. Gail would bring
her home a nice fat slug and Edwina
would eat it regally – one gulp and it

was gone. She did not say much now. She seemed to be brooding. Gail wondered what the frog was thinking about.

She soon found out.

One morning Mum came into the kitchen and said, "You know what I found in the bedroom? A frog. It must have been sitting at the foot of the bed all night."

Rupert turned pale. "What did you do with it?"

"What d'you think? Took it down

the garden and chucked it into the
pond."

That afternoon, Gail found
Edwina on the flannel, breathing
heavily. She seemed worn out. She
didn't say much but looked sly. After
that Gail kept window and door
shut.

But a few days later, Mum said,
"Gail, love. You're to leave your
room door open. It's stuffy in there."

"I don't want anyone going in,"

said Gail. Then added to herself, "or coming out."

"Well, the room'll need cleaning, girl."

"I'll do it myself."

"Are you all right, Gail?"

"Don't be sarky, Mum."

One afternoon that week, Rupert was working late and Aunt Mandy was round.

As Mum poured the tea she said, "You know that flaming frog's at it again."

Aunt Mandy looked at Mum, then at Gail.

"That's the second time I've found it squatting at the end of our bed. Been there all night. What's up?" Mum began to stare at both of them.

Aunt Mandy had spilt her tea. Gail had gone red. Mum went out for the dish cloth and Aunt Mandy said quickly, "Gail, love. D'you know 'owt about this frog?"

Gail took a deep breath and nodded.

"Is it a – lady frog?"

Gail nodded again. Mum came back with the cloth.

"What are you two on about?"

Aunt Mandy stood up. "Jackie.

Now listen to me. Do what I tell you
and don't argue."

Mum and Gail stared, baffled.

"Get a change of clothes for
Rupert. I'll pick him up from the
Club when he finishes and take
him on to my place. He mustn't
sleep here any more." She looked
at Mum's face, then added, "For
a bit."

Mum hesitated then went upstairs.

Gail burst out, "What's going on
Aunt Mandy?"

"I thought you knew all about
these things, Gail. Look, if this
frog-woman . . ."

"Edwina, you mean."

Aunt Mandy stared. "Edwina? Oh
yes. If Edwina gets to sleep three

times at the foot of the Prince's bed,
then he is hers."

"Oh no!" Gail shrieked,
remembering all the stories Aunt
Mandy had told her.

Mum came back into the room
with a small case.

"Now, what's it all about?"

Aunt Mandy took the case.

"No time to explain. You won't
regret this Jackie, honest."

And with that Aunt Mandy left,
giving Gail a quick wink as she went.

Chapter Five

For a few days there was no sign of
Edwina. Then Gail found her
squatting on the flannel, looking
baleful.

"Where has Rupert gone?" she
demanded.

Gail shrugged.

"This Aunt Mandy of yours,"
went on Edwina, "must be a witch."

"Don't know what you're talking
about."

"You do, Gail, you do. And I
thought you were my friend. I

thought we were girls together,"
wheedled Edwina.

Gail laughed, cruelly.

"You what? Girls together? You're
a stuck-up madam. And a stirrer as
well. Just because someone decided
you were marrying Rupert when you
were both in infant school – you
can't hold him to that now."

"You understand nothing, girl.
Rupert and I are destined for each
other. Do not stand in our way."

Edwina swelled up. Gail tried not
to laugh.

"By the way, where does Aunt
Mandy live?" Edwina asked
suddenly.

"Town Road," said Gail without
thinking.

"Thank you, my dear." Edwina was triumphant.

Gail made a dive for her but the frog was out of the window in a flash. Gail bit her lip. From now on it was down to Aunt Mandy.

Chapter Six

Next day, Aunt Mandy phoned. "Gail. Can't you keep your mouth shut for two minutes together?"

"Sorry," muttered Gail.

"Listen. I'm moving him to a bed and breakfast. I'm not telling you or your mum. He can stay there till this blows over."

"But, what about his job?"

"Don't worry. He's going to be ill for a week or two."

Days passed. At school the tadpole-frogs got bigger, their legs

grew longer, their tails shorter. At
home, Gail got more excited and her
mum got more depressed.

One evening came a knock on the
door. It was the Manager of the
Bingo Club.

"Rupert," he said. "Is he – like – all right?"

"He's away," said Mum, going red. "He's ill."

"I know. I've been sent a sick note. It says he's suffering from Ranophobia."

"What?" gasped Mum, going pale.

"I looked it up," said the Manager. "It means 'fear of frogs'. So I'm a bit worried. The club members miss him, you see."

"Oh, he'll be back. Don't worry," said Gail confidently. But she didn't feel confident.

A week went by. The little frogs were swarming all over the artificial rocks in the aquarium. Miss reckoned they

were almost ready for the pond.

At home the atmosphere grew
more tense. When, one evening the
vicar turned up on the doorstep,
Mum nearly passed out.

"This very nice young man," he
said, "Rupert – ah Prince, came to
see me."

"Oh," said Mum, blushing scarlet.
"Is he all right?"

"That was what I was going to
ask," said the vicar. "Before he left
the vicarage, he asked me to check

if there were any frogs in my
garden."

"Well," said Mum, "he does have
a bit of a thing about frogs. But does
that have anything to do with you?"

"Ah," smiled the vicar. "It has a
lot to do with me. You see he wants
to marry you – very soon. A full-scale
wedding with bells."

"Bells?"

"He insisted on bells. I felt I must
see you. I needed to know if you were
happy about the idea."

"I'm ecstatic," said Mum.

Next morning, Gail woke to find
Edwina lying exhausted on the
flannel. Her voice was low.

"I give up. I'm beaten. She's

welcome to him. He was a pompous ass anyway."

"He'd never have married you, even if you changed back into a princess," jeered Gail.

"Changed back!" shrieked Edwina. "Who wanted to change back? I wanted to change him."

"You what?" Now Gail was shrieking.

"Yes, idiot child. I wanted us both to be frogs." Edwina's voice grew stronger. "Ah, to swim together in the green depths, to frolic among the slime and weeds."

She stopped. "Princess indeed. People don't appreciate Royalty any more – but frogs. Do you know, Gail, in Town Road they held up the traffic for me to go over the crossing. There's respect for you."

Edwina recovered her bounce. Her voice became friendly.

"Tell you what, love. Give's a lift back to Maggie's pond, will t'a?"

Gail got up. "Are you sure? You wanted to get away from there before."

"I know, dear. But I hear there's a new intake; fresh young frogs, some very handsome ones by all accounts."

Gail laughed. She pulled the bucket out of the cupboard, wet the flannel again and dropped it in.

"All aboard," she shouted.

Mum called up from the kitchen.
"You all right, Gail?"

"Never better, Mum," she
answered.

It was a lovely wedding, bells and
all. Gail was bridesmaid, Aunt
Mandy was Best Woman and the
Bingo Manager gave the bridegroom
away.

And they all lived happily ever
after – sort of.